MY GREATEST MISTAKE

A Work of Fiction

Comfort Ibeh Agbanyim

MY GREATEST MISTAKE

A Work of Fiction

Contents

DEDICATION

This book is dedicated to my lovely parents Mr. and Mrs. J. Ibeh Agbanyim for being the best parents on earth.

ACKNOWLEDGEMENTS

All thanks to God for giving me the strength to write this book. I appreciate Mrs. Miriam Ukporo my class teacher for her invaluable support and encouragement. Also to Miss Dorcas Christopher for her effort in complying and making this book a success. I love and celebrate you all.

CAST

- MARTIN MAIN CHARACTER
- VERONICA MARTIN'S WIFE
- SOFIA MARTIN'S DAUGHTER
- DANIEL MARTIN'S SON
- ISABELLA MARTIN'S SECRETARY
- NICHOLAS ISABELLA'S FIANCÉ
- GEORGE VERONICA'S FATHER
- STEPHANIE VERONICA'S MOTHER
- VICTOR POLICE OFFICER
- CHRIS VICTOR'S ASSISTANT
- FELICIA VICTOR'S WIFE
- THOMAS NICHOLAS'S FATHER
- ANTONIA NICHOLAS's MOTHER

All the actions of this play take place in Miami, Florida U.S.A. The time is in the 21st century

ACT ONE

SCENE ONE

(At Martin's house, a well-furnished apartment with three rooms, around 9:00pm, we see veronica sitting on the couch watching television and then the door opens and Martin's walks in).

Veronica: *(Still sitting)* why are you just coming back by this time?

Martins: Is that how to welcome your husband who just came back from work.

Veronica: *(stands up and turns to martin)*. Why should I welcome you? *(in an angry tone)*, it seems like you've forgotten that you're a married man with a family and you shouldn't be coming back home by this time, so tell me what's your excuse for coming home late.

Martin:	(*Drops his bag on the couch while talking to her*) I had much work to do today, are you happy now?
Veronica:	That's not true, what amount of work will you have that will make you come back home late? You came back home 1 late because of Isabella. I'm sure that both of you had so much to talk about that you forgot that you have a family.
Martin:	Listen; I'm not in the mood to put up with your nagging today (*Walks to the kitchen*).
Veronica:	(*She follows him while talking*) so I'm now a nagging wife huh? Just because I'm asking my husband why he came back home late, you're calling me a nagging wife.
Martins:	(*Looks around the kitchen*) where's my food?
Veronica:	Don't change the topic; tell me the truth, why did you come back home this late?
Martin:	(*Increases his tone*) I've already told you why I came back by this time, what else do you want me to say. I walked into my own house and my wife didn't even greet me and then I walked into the kitchen, there's no food for me to eat and now I have to put up with you nagging me every day.

Veronica: You know what, make your food by yourself *(She leaves the kitchen and walks into her room)*

Martin: (Walks into the parlor and sits down on the couch) my family is falling apart, my own wife does not even respect me anymore (Shake his head) what am I going to do? (Sighs heavily).

(He turns off the television and walks into his room)
(Lights Fade)

ACT ONE

SCENE TWO

(Lights open on Isabella and Nicholas in a fancy restaurant having dinner together).

Nicholas: I'm sure you don't know the main reason why I asked you to have dinner with me.

Isabella: What do you mean the main reason; I taught you asked me to have dinner with you so that we can just talk.

Nicholas: No, I asked you to have dinner with me because I want to take our relationship to the next level.

Isabella: To the next level?

Nicholas: Yes (puts his hand into his pocket and brings out an engagement ring. He kneels down) Will you marry me?

Isabella: (*Looking surprised*) marry you?

Nicholas: Yes

Isabella: Isn't it too soon

Nicholas: What do you mean too soon, we've been dating for three years? Don't you think it's time for us to make it official?

Isabella: Yes but....

Nicholas: But what!

Isabella: (*Sighs*) ok, yes

Nicholas: Seriously?

Isabella: (*Smiling*) yes

Nicholas: (*He puts ring in her finger, and both of them stood up and hugged*)

(*Lights Fade*)

ACT ONE

SCENE THREE

(Lights open on Martin in his office, a well furnish office with modern equipment and three paintings on the wall). Isabella walks in with some files in her hands).

Isabella: Sir, these are the files you requested for *(Martin seems lost and not paying attention to what she is saying)* Sir,

Martin: Sorry, where you saying something?

Isabella: Yes Sir, these are the files you requested for *(He collects the files from her)* Sir are you ok? Is everything alright?

Martin: Yes

Isabella: Sir, are you sure?

Martin: (*Sighs*) well, actually no, nothing is fine (*Pauses*) you know what, have a seat let's talk (*She sits down on one of the chairs in front of his table*). I get so much respect in the office but when I get home my wife keeps nagging me and disrespects me. I have had enough. I could have divorced her a long time ago but I can't because of my kids. if I do it would be traumatizing for my kids (*Shakes his head*).

Isabella: I'm so sorry Sir, I didn't know you were going through a lot at home and here I am disturbing you with work.

Martin: There's no need for the apology you didn't do anything, you were just doing your job that's all.

Isabella: (*She stands up*) Sir my sincere apologies for any inconveniences. I'll go back to work now, oh! And if you need anything just let me know.

Martin: Ok thank you so much for listening to me

Isabella: You are welcome Sir.

(*Lights Fade*)

ACT ONE

SCENE FOUR

(In the evening, Isabella is having dinner with Nicholas's family; he introduced her to his family as his fiancé).

Nicholas:	You told me we were going to meet someone very special to you but you didn't tell us who she was because you wanted it to be a surprise hum?
Nicholas:	Yes Dad I'll like to introduce someone to you (*Isabella walks in*) Dad, Mum I'd like you to meet Isabella I told you about her once but I think it's time that you meet her in person.
Isabella:	Good evening ma, good evening Sir
Antonia:	Good evening my dear, please have a sit so that we can have dinner together and you can tell us about yourself. (*Nicholas pulls the chair backwards so that Isabella can sit*).

Thomas:	So, tell us about yourself what do you do for a living. I mean, do you live alone or with your parents.
Nicholas:	Dad, that's a lot of questions which one do you expect her to answer first.
Isabella:	No, its ok I'll answer all of them. There's no problem. Actually I'm a secretary in the International Finance Bank. I live alone. I am an orphan my parents died 5 years ago in a ghastly motor accident.
Antonia:	I'm so sorry
Isabella:	Its ok, I'm already used to it
Thomas:	I'm so sorry for reminding you of your past. It's just that he's my only son and I want him to get married to a good girl. I'm not saying that you a bad girl/lady. It's actually the opposite you're really nice lady and I believe that you are the right person for my son. Honey what do you think?
Antonia:	Well, yes that's true, you're a nice, beautiful and you have a good job. You seem to be perfect for my son.
Isabella:	Thank you ma, thank you so much for the compliments.
Antonia:	You deserve it my dear

Nicholas: I know you were going to like her

One Hour Later
(Every One Is Done eating)

Nicholas: (*Standing*) I think it's time for us to go.

Isabella: Yea I think so (*Standing*) (*Antonia and Thomas Stand up*) it was really nice meeting you.

Antonia: Yes, it was nice to meet you too.

(They all hug each other)
(Lights Fade)

ACT ONE

SCENE FIVE

(Nicholas is taking Isabella home and they have a discussion)

Nicholas: You haven't told me how your day went.

Isabella: Well it was good but Mr. Martin told me something that makes me feel sorry for him.

Nicholas: How do you mean? Please explain

Isabella: Throughout today Mr. Martin was very moody and I understand that he is really suffering in his own home. His wife doesn't even respect him anymore. He told me he wanted to divorce her but he can't because of his kids.

Nicholas: But I don't understand what that has to do with you

Isabella: How do you mean? He just told me because he wanted to confide in someone.

Nicholas: So you were the only person he could confide in. Why didn't he meet a therapist?

Isabella: I can't believe you, I just told you what my boss is passing through, you don't even seem to sympathize him.

Nicholas: I feel sorry for him, it's just that I don't get why he had to tell you, wasn't there any other person around there he could tell?

Isabella: You know what, you're so insensitive. I just told you what happened to my boss and you're throwing a jealous fit.

Nicholas: I'm not jealous; I just don't understand why he told you, how close are you to your boss?

Isabella: We're just friends that's all, I'm not very close to him

Nicholas: Are you sure?

Isabella: Yes, there's no need for you to be jealous alright, we're engaged and we'll soon get married and be happy. Let's just put all this behind us ok.

Nicholas: (*Sighs*) ok fine

(They reach her house and she gets down from the car)

Nicholas: How about picking you up tomorrow, what do you think?

Isabella: Hmmm

Nicholas: Please

Isabella: Ok

Nicholas: Bye, see you tomorrow then

Isabella: Yes, Bye

(She walks into the house)
(Lights Fade)

ACT ONE

SCENE SIX

(At Martin's house, Veronica is in the kitchen dishing out food, Martin walks into the house), Veronica leaves the kitchen and goes into the living room to see Martin)

Veronica: Good evening

Martin: Good evening

Veronica: You came back home on time today, let me guess, Isabella had somewhere to go, so she left early and you decide to come home early.

Martin: Won't you ever be tired of nagging? What of the kids

Veronica: They are asleep.

Martin: Ok (*Loosens his tie and keeps his bag on an couch*)

Veronica: So you're uncomfortable discussion about Isabella huh? Is there any specific reason?

14

Martin: (*Increases his tone*) that's enough, I can't take this anymore, every time I come back you keep on nagging me with the same issue, aren't you ever tired of disturbing my peace. Can't I ever come home and have peace of mind? When I come back home late you complain, when I come back home early, you complain you can never allow me to rest.

Veronica: Peace of mind? Well, if you don't have peace of mind at home why don't you just go to Isabella house and have peace there if you want.

(Martin raises his hand to hit her)

Veronica: Well, you want to hit me, go ahead, do it!; then maybe you will finally be happy. (*Martin drops his hand*) why didn't you do it?

Martin: Because I'm not a coward and I don't hit women but one of these days if you keep on provoking me I might run out of patience with you. Good night (*Walks into his room*).

Veronica: (*Soliloquies*) Isabella, if I find out that there's something going on between you my husband, I promise you will pay for it dearly.

(Lights fade)

ACT TWO

SCENE ONE

(At Martin's house, Martin is still asleep while Veronica, Sofia and Daniel are having breakfast. Then, he wakes up takes his shower he walks into the living room).

Veronica: Good morning

Martin: Good morning

Sofia &

Daniel: Daddy good morning

Martin: Good morning kids, the food looks delicious *(Sits down)* so tell me Daniel how was school yesterday, did you do all your home work?

Daniel: Yes, mum helped us.

Martin: That's great *(Turns to Veronica)* why didn't the alarm ring around six o'clock

Veronica: I turned it off

17

Martin: Why did you turn it off?

Veronica: I turned it off because it's always too loud and noisy and disturbs me whenever it rings.

Martin: Well, why didn't you tell me before you turned it off?

Veronica: I didn't think it was necessary.

Martin: You know that it's thanks to that alarm that I wake up early to go to work. You should have at least told me before you turned it off. Now I'm going to be late to work today.

Veronica: I'm sorry then, next time I'll ask you before I do that.

Martin: Yeah, I'll really appreciate.

Daniel: Mum, I'm done eating.

Veronica: Ok, go to your room and pack your backpack.

Daniel: Yes mum (*Stands up and goes to his room*)

Martin: (*Turns to Sofia*) so, tell me princess how was school yesterday did you learn new things?

Sofia: Yes dad I learnt about living and non-ling things.

Martin: Really? That's nice; tell me what are living things?

Sofia: Living things are things that have life in them.

Martin: That's good, have you done your homework?

Sofia: Yes dad, mum helped me.

Martin: Ok.

Sofia: Mum, I'm done with my food thank you dad, thank you mum.

Veronica: Ok, go to your room and pack your backpack with your brother.

Sofia: Ok mum.

Martin: I might come back home early today because I don't have so much work to do. I'm just telling you because I don't want you to start questioning me if I come back early and I'm sorry for almost hitting you yesterday. You know I'm not like that, I was really upset, I'm really sorry. Will you forgive me?

Veronica:	I'll think about it, you've never raised your hand on me before; I was surprised when you did that last night.
Martin:	I'm sorry; it's just that I hate it when you question me.
Veronica:	Oh yeah? Or you hate when I talk about Isabella.
Martin:	Oh, come on not again with the same topic. How many times do I have to tell you that there's nothing going on between Isabella and I.
Veronica:	Well, it's a pity because I didn't believe you.
Martin:	That's your problem; I've told you what I have to say. If you don't believe me that's your business and besides; why did you think there'd ever be anything between us.
Veronica:	Well, is because she is beautiful, nice and intelligent.
Martin:	So you're jealous of her.
Veronica:	Of course not.
Martin:	So why do you keep on insisting that there's something between us.

Veronica: It's because I just know it, I feel it and besides I know when you are lying to me and when you're not.

Martin: (*Laughs*). You know what, you're so unbelievable, (He stands up and leaves) oh! Thanks for the food.

Veronica: You're welcome

(Veronica carries the dishes into the kitchen and walks out of his room)

Daniel: Mum, I'm done packing.

Veronica: Is your sister done? (*Sofia walks out of the room*)

Sofia: Yes mum.

Veronica: Dad is taking you to school today.

(Martin walks into the living room dressed in his suit)

Martin: Kids let's go.

Daniel: Who will pick us from school?

Martin: Your mum is going to pick you today and you will spend the night at your grandpa's house.

Daniel: Ok, dad

(They leave the stage)
(Lights fade)

ACT TWO

SCENE TWO

(Lights open on Inspector Victor having breakfast with his wife Felicia)

Felicia: How was work yesterday? I noticed you came back late.

ASP Victor: I'm sorry; it's just that Chris and I are working on a case of a man who constantly raped his stepdaughter. She told one of her teachers and they reported him, but we can't arrest him because we don't have enough evidence against him. So we are thinking of a way of catching him red handed. Do you have any idea?

Felicia: Well, I hate people that take advantage of those who can't defend themselves. From my opinion, I think you should install cameras in those places where he rapes her if he does it again; you arrest him in the act.

ASP Victor: (*Nods*) I think that's a good idea, I wonder why I didn't think of this before now. You're a genius, that's exactly what we're going to do. In fact, let me call Chris right now and tell him.

Felecia: (*Smiling*) thanks for the compliments.

ASP Victor: You' re welcome.

(*The phone rings at Chris' house and he picks it up*).

INSP Chris: Hello.

ASP Victor: Hello, Chris how are you?

INSP Chris: I'm fine, please who is this?

ASP Victor: What do you mean who is this? This is your boss, Victor

INSP Chris: Oh! I'm sorry sir, good evening; you called me on my landline so I didn't know who it was.

ASP Victor: Yeah, I called your cell phone but you didn't answer, I had to call your landline.

INSP Chris: Yes sir, I'm sorry my cell phone was charging, so I didn't hear it.

ASP Victor: That's ok; actually I want you to tell you that my genius wife just came up with a great idea for us to catch that rapist.

INSP Chris: Really? What did she come up with?

ASP Victor: She suggested that we should install some cameras in the rooms where he normally rapes her so that when he does it again, we will have proof against him and then arrest him.

INSP Chris: That's a good idea. Sir, we can't install the cameras in the room by ourselves he'll know that we're police officers.

ASP Victor: That's right, (pauses) what if we give the cameras to the girl to install.

INSP Chris: I don't think that's really a good idea what if he catches her.

ASP Victor: Yeah, what if we tell her to install the cameras at night, when everybody is fast asleep.

INSP Chris: That will be great then.

ASP Victor: Ok, will do everything today, so that we can finally catch that criminal.

INSP Chris: Ok, sir

25

ASP Victor: We'll meet at the office.

INSP Chris: Bye (*Victor hangs up*)

Felicia: You're going to carry out everything today?

ASP Victor: Don't worry, I've dealt with more dangerous criminals and nothing has happened to me. I'll be fine, as long as I have the grace of God with me, I'll be fine.

Felicia: I'll pray for you.

ASP Victor: Thank you. (*He is done eating*) Thanks for the food. (*He stands up*) Bye, I'm leaving now.

Felicia: Bye, Good luck (he leaves and she clears all the plates).

(Lights fade)

ACT TWO

SCENE THREE

(At Daniel and Sofia's school, Veronica comes to pick them up. They run and hug her).

Veronica: Hello, my prince and princess how was school today?

Daniel: School was great. We learnt lots of things.

Veronica: Really?

Sofia: Yes mum.

Veronica: Ok, how about you tell me on our way to grandpas' house.

(They enter a yellow colored taxi and the taxi drives away)
(Lights fade)

ACT TWO

SCENE FOUR

(At Martins office, Martin is discussing with his boss, Pedro he is telling him that all the loans he gave had gone bad and his job is on the line).

Martin: Good afternoon Sir.

Pedro: I don't know what's so good about this afternoon; did you know that the loans you gave to customers went bad? This company is losing a lot of money and your job is on the line. If this company goes bankrupt your job here is over.

Martin: What! Sir I don't understand what you mean that they aren't repaying their loans.

Pedro: That's right, they aren't repaying their loans. Most of them have one excuse or the other for not paying up their loans. I'm advising you as your boss and a friend do something to save this company, because if you don't, you'll be fired.

Martin: But, sir I don't know what you expect me to do.

Pedro: Listen, you've got to think of something, just come up with something, but make sure all the loans are repaid.

Martin: I'll try my best sir.

Pedro: Don't try your best, do your best and make sure your best is successful. You get that?

Martin: Yes sir.

Pedro: That's if you still want to work here. Excuse me (he stands and leaves).

Martin: Go ahead sir (*He sighs heavily*).

(Lights fade)

ACT TWO

SCENE FIVE

(Martin walks into his house around 10:00pm looking depressed. Veronica is standing at the door waiting for him)

Martin: *(In a sad low tone)* why are you standing there?

Veronica: I was waiting for my husband to come back late as he always does.

Martin: Listen, Veronica, right now I'm in a really bad mood because of what just happened at work today. My boss told me that all the loans that I gave to customers have gone bad because they aren't repaying the loan and that the company funds dropping; and that my job is on the line. So, please just spare me your nagging *(Walks into the room)*.

Veronica: *(She follows him)* and so what, you can just get a new job. You're a great accountant and you can use your certificate to find a new job, that isn't enough reason why you should come back late.

Martin: (*Stops and turns to her*) are you stupid (*Increases his tone*) do you think it's that easy to find a job? Is it because I provide you with everything you need and you don't have to work and then think that jobs grow on trees you can just go and pluck it hun!, listen if I get fired and I go to find another job, do you think they'll hire me, because they'll be wondering why I got fired and they'll think that I'm not a good bank manager. Do you understand it now?

Veronica: I don't care about whatever that happens to you at work all I know is that you'll find a new job, I want to know the real reason why you came back home this late, were you with Isabella? (*Shouts at her*).

Martin: Do you know that you're a selfish, nagging and annoying woman? For the past few months, you've been so unbearable. I would have divorced you long time ago if not for the kids. I just can't take it anymore! (*Veronica slaps him*)

Veronica: How dare you call me a selfish woman. I've been putting up with your late coming and disrespect. You're a useless and disrespectful man. (*Martin slaps her so hard that she falls to the ground*).

31

Martin:	Don't you ever insult me again. I've done everything I can to keep this family together but it's impossible with you (*Pauses*) I'm sorry, I'm so so sorry. Get up. (*Veronica is not responding, she is still lying on the ground*) Please stand. Veronica are you ok? (He kneels and tries to carry her, He carries her head and sees the blood on the floor) oh! no! no!! no!!! no!!!! no!!!! (*He stands and rushes to the bathroom, takes cup of water and sprinkles it on her*) My God! (*He looks scared, he is shivering and his heart rate rises, he rushes out of the room and runs into the living room, he picks up his phone and calls Isabella.*) Please pick up come on.......

(The phone rings at Isabella's house when she is with her fiancé, she stands up and goes to answer the phone she picks it up).

Isabella:	Hello
Martin:	(*In a low tone*) hello, Isabella.
Isabella:	Oh, hello Mr. Martin what's wrong, why are you talking in a low tone.
Martin:	It's nothing the thing is that I'll like to borrow your car.

Isabella: Borrow my car? How about yours

Martin: Well, they thing is that it's at a mechanic workshop and I want to go and collect some files from the office.

Isabella: Sir, but can't you collect them tomorrow?

Martin: No I can't the thing is that I need them tonight because I want to compile some information.

Isabella: Ok Sir I'll come to your house and give it to you.

Martin: No, I'll rather come to your house and collect it.

Isabella: Ok, then how is your wife

Martin: She's fine, thank you,

(she hangs up Nicholas is standing behind her)

Nicholas: Who was that?

Isabella: (*Shakes*) Ah! You scared me?

Nicholas: I'm sorry, who was that?

Isabella:	It was my boss
Nicholas:	You're boss?
Isabella:	Yes, he asked me to lend him my car so that he can go to the office and collect some files.
Nicholas:	This late? Why not tomorrow
Isabella:	He said he needed the files for some information tonight. So I just had to lend him my car.
Nicholas:	Well, ok but something seems weird.
Isabella:	Let's finish our dinner; he'll be here soon
Nicholas:	Ok

(Martin rushes out of the house and enters a taxi to Isabella's house).
(Lights fade)

ACT THREE

SCENE ONE

(Martin arrives at Isabella's house and presses the doorbell; Nicholas opens the door)

Nicholas: May I help you?

Isabella: (*Walking towards the door*) Who is it? Oh! Good evening Mr. Martin.

Martin: God evening Isabella, I'm sorry but I've not met him.

Isabella: Oh! Yes Mr. Martin, this is Nicholas, my fiancé

Nicholas: Nice to meet you (*Martin and Nicholas shake hands*)

Martin: Nice to meet you too

Isabella: Come in.

Martin: No thanks, I'd rather just take the car and leave. (*Isabella goes into the house to bring the keys*)

Nicholas: So, you're the famous Martin

Martin: Famous! I'm not a celebrity.

Nicholas: I know, it's just that my fiancé has told me a lot about you, she told me about what is happening between you and your wife.

Martin: Really?

Nicholas: Yeah, she told me everything, I'm sorry, speaking of her, how is she?

Martin: She's fine

Nicholas: That's good

(Isabella comes out and gives the key to Martin)

Martin: Thank you

Isabella: You're welcome

Martin: Bye.

Isabella: Bye.

Nicholas: Bye.

(They close the door and go in sharp black out)
(Lights fade)

ACT THREE

SCENE TWO

(Martin arrives at his house with Isabella's car. He goes into the house and put's Veronica's body in a big carton. He puts the carton into the car and drives off, he is sweating and very restless, he drives for about thirty minutes. Then he parked the car in a lonely forest with a river nearby. He throws the body into the river and drives back home. At home he takes a rag and cleans the bloodstains on the floor of his room).

(Lights fade)

ACT THREE

SCENE THREE

(Lights open on Martin, George and Stephanie in George's house).

Stephanie: *(Comes out of the room)* Daniel and Sofia are coming.

Martin: OK

George: Where is Veronica?

Martin: What do you mean where Veronica is? I thought she came here.

Stephanie: Yes she did, but to drop the kids, since then we've not seen her.

Martin: She didn't tell you?

George: Tell us what?

Martin: She told me that after dropping the kid, that she'll tell you goodbye because she is travelling to.

Stephanie: What?

Martin: Seriously, she didn't tell you?

George: No, She didn't say anything

Martin: She didn't come last night, so I thought she already left

Stephanie: Oh No, what if she did something crazy

George: No, you're just over reacting may be she's with her friends, let's call some of her friends.

Stephanie: (*Picks up the phone and calls Veronica's friend*) Hello, how are you, I just called to ask you if Veronica is with you. She's not with you, ok thank you Bye. (*Turns to Martin*) she's not there.

George: Let's call her other friend. (He picks up the phone and calls one of Veronica's friends). Hello, how are you? I'm good. I called to ask you if you have seen Veronica. You've not? No, Ok, thanks bye. (puts down the phone) she's not there either.

Stephanie: My veronica, I just hope she is fine and safe

George: I think we should report this to the police, Martin what do you think?

Martin: Yes, I totally agree, let's go (*David and Sofia run out of the room and hug Martins*).

Daniel: Where's mum?

Martin: Your mum went out. She'll be back

Sofia: Daddy!

Martin: How are you princess?

Sofia: I'm fine daddy.

Daniel: Dad, where are you going?

Martin: Your grandpa and I are going somewhere. We will be back soon.

Stephanie: I'm coming with you.

George: No, stay here in case she calls and watch the kids

Stephanie: Ok

Martin: (*Stands up*) ok let's go George

(They leave the stage)
(Lights fade)

ACT THREE

SCENE FOUR

(Martin and George walk into ASP Victors' office & Insp. Chris is there too)

Martin: Good morning Sir.

ASP Victor: Good morning, please have a seat.

George: We'll like to make a complain, of a missing person

ASP Victor: Who is she?

Martin: She is my wife

George: And she's my daughter, her name is Veronica

Asp Victor: Since when has she been missing?

Martin: Since yesterday

Asp Victor: (*The Phone rings*) excuse me, hello, ok, thank you (*He hangs up*) A body has just been found in the lake around the forest and traces of a grey SUV Car that belongs to Isabella Lorenzo. We will like you to identify the body and see if it's Mrs. Veronica. (*They left his office*) Which one of your wants to identify the body?

Martin: I'll do it

George: Are you sure?

Martin: Yeah, wait here for me I'll be right back

(Martin leaves with the inspector and goes into a large room with about 20 corpses lying on a stroller they reached Veronica's body, he open its)

ASP Victor: Is she the one?

Martin: Yes, She's the one

(Martin walks out sobbing)

George: It's not Veronica right? Please tell me it's not Veronica.

43

Martin: I'm so sorry but she's the one

George: (*He breaks down crying*) No, Not my Veronica.

ASP Victor: Mr. Martin, you're going to follow me for questioning.

Martin: Ok.

(He walks into the interrogation room and Asp victor begins to question him).

ASP Victor: Where were you last night?

Martin: At home.

Asp Victor: What time did you get back from work last night?

Martin: Around 10pm

ASP Victor: How was your relationship with your wife?

Martin: It was like every other couple relationship, we had some argument, and we resolved it and we loved each other so much.

Asp Victor: When was the last time you saw your wife?

Martin:	It was yesterday morning.
Asp Victor:	During your arguments was there any violence involved.
Martin:	Of course not; we just argued. There was no violence.
Asp Victor:	I don't have any other questions for you. You can leave now.
Martin:	Thank you.

(He leaves the room and walks up to George)

Martin:	George, you're going to have to go home on your own I have some work to do.
George:	Ok.

(He leaves the station Martins calls Isabella and asks her to meet him at a restaurant).
(Lights fade)

ACT THREE

SCENE FIVE

(At Nice Restaurant, Martin and Isabella are discussing)

Martin: Before anything I want you to know that I care about you so much and I will never want anything bad to happen to you.

Isabella: You're scaring me, why are you saying all this.

Martin: Remember yesterday night that I borrowed your car.

Isabella: Yes I do

Martin: I'm sure you know my wife was murdered

Isabella: I'm so sorry that's so sad

Martin: It's ok. The truth is that I murdered my wife but it was an accident. Yesterday I came back home, my wife started nagging as usual but the difference was that yesterday I was angry because my work was threatened so she insulted me and then slapped me, I got very angry that I slapped her back, she fell and hit her head on the floor and died. So I used your car to carry her corpse and threw her in the lake, but they found it and they found traces of your car so they want to arrest you.

Isabella: Please let me get this straight, you murdered your wife accidentally and used my car to carry her, now they found out my car was there and the cops are after me.

Martin: Yes I'm really sorry I didn't mean to put you in trouble.

Isabella: I believe you and I know that you are a good man.

Martins: Thank you for believing in me. I told you because I wanted you to know what mess I got you into. I'm very sorry.

Isabella: Its' ok I forgive you (*Both stand*)

Martin: Oh! This is the greatest mistake I have ever made in life. Bye.

Isabella: Bye.

(Lights fade)

ACT THREE

SCENE SIX

(Isabella is arrested and interrogated at the police station).

ASP Victor: We know that your car was at the forest where Mrs Veronica body was found.

Isabella: So, what do I have to do with it.

ASP Victor: Tell us why you were at the forest at that time and tell us the whole truth.

Isabella: (Pauses, then sighs heavily) ok, fine, Mr. Martin called me last night and told me that, he wants to borrow my car because his car was at the mechanic workshop. I agree, he told me wants to go to the office and collect some files but he lied to me. Mr. Martin actually killed his wife, but it was an accident, so he took my car so that he can cover up his act by throwing his wife's corpse into the lake.

Asp Victor: When did you find out all these?

Isabella: Today, he told me everything was an accident

Asp Victor: Take her away (*Insp Chris detains Isabella, Asp victor goes to Martins house to arrest Martins*).

(Lights fade)

ACT THREE

SCENE SEVEN

(Martin is arrested and interrogated at the police stations)

Asp Victor: Isabella already told us everything. Say your own version of the incident and why you murdered your wife.

Martin: I came back home and my wife and I had an argument. She slapped me and I got very angry that I hit her so hard that she fell on the ground. Sir this is my first time of hitting her.

Asp Victor: And you expect me to believe you, your neighbors said that two of you always argue.

Martin: Yes, I won't deny that but I will say this again that I've never hit her before. That was the first time.

ASP Victor: I'll make sure you have the maximum sentence. How could you murder the mother of your kids? Didn't you even think of your kids before you did that?

Martin: It was an accident!!

ASP Victor: Take him away

Martin: It was an accident! It was an accident. (*He was taken away and detained*).

(Lights fade)

ACT FOUR

SCENE ONE

Martin's trial approached and the judge sentenced him to life imprisonment for the murder of his wife but that he could be released earlier based on good behavior, his kids forgave him and understood that he didn't kill their mum intentionally it was an accident. Isabella and Nicholas got married and had three children, George and Stephanie got over the death of their daughter and forgave Martin and they lived happily ever after.

THE END

About The Author

Comfort Ibeh Agbanyim is currently a 9th Grader. She has received several recognitions for her teamwork abilities and outstanding academic performance. She was awarded the Best Student in Citizenship course in 2013; a Class Prefect position in 8th grade; received a scholarship for her excellent academic performance; and a Certificate of Appreciation for her participation in A Celebration of Peace event at Lions Club International.

Comfort is athletic. She enjoys track running, soccer and volleyball. She aspires to study medicine and specializes in pediatric.

www.ingramcontent.com/pod-product-compliance
Lightning Source LLC
Chambersburg PA
CBHW022053170626
46808CB00003B/1456